MORE ___ WITH STICK MAN TRUM

Eric (the Stick Man) Trum
Jonny Staples

'The woods would be quiet if no bird sang but the one that sang best.'

- Henry van Dyke

Well hello there, I'm Eric (the stick man) Trum.

Stop !!!!

I think I just saw you looking at my bottom!
Hmmmmmmm?!?!

Well, this could be a good time to let you know
that I'd rather you didn't look at it in any of the
pictures in this book.

Yes I know.... I have an unusually large bum for a stick man, and I know people like to look at it, but I'm a little bit embarrassed about it, so please don't peek. If you feel the need to look, just move your eyes so they are looking at my rather pleasant face instead. Thank you.

So, now that we've got that sorted that out I'll tell you a little bit more about me.

I actually started life as a doodle. Yes, at the beginning I was just a little drawing in Jonny's funny doodle book surrounded by all kinds of other strange

6

pictures. Soon after he'd drawn me, I came alive, which was extremely strange and we were both rather surprised. None of Jonny's other drawings have ever come alive so I suppose I'm a bit special really.

Luckily Jonny and I got on quite well and we've been having a lot of fun ever since meeting on that doodle book, four months ago.

Overall I have a pretty good life as Jonny is always finding me fun things to do, my only real problem is my bottom; in fact this large bottom of mine has caused me a lot of problems over the last few months. Even as recently as last week I've been having 'bum issues'.

The most recent incident occurred while I was using Jonny's teapot as a playground last week. I climbed to the top of the spout and was just about to slide down it when I got stuck! It was very awkward and Jonny had to carry me around the house, attached to the teapot for nearly a week.

'Well at least there's a handle,' he said as he moved me from room to room.

I watched TV from the teapot, ate my lunch from the teapot and even slept hanging out of the end of the teapot. (And don't even ask about going to the toilet!) In the end Jonny had to break it to get me out! He was very upset when he looked at all the smashed bits of pottery lying on the floor.

'I think we'll have to go to town on the bus tomorrow and choose a new one,' he said as he picked up the broken pieces. He put all the fragments in his 'useful things' box (which is full of things that

will never be useful), and sat down to look at the bus timetable.

I'd never been to town before and was rather excited. I tried to do a cartwheel to celebrate, but because of my heavy bottom, I crashed to the floor half way through it.

The next day I got up very early to get ready for

the big day out. I had an extra big breakfast, which

included a cornflake covered with jelly, and I made a

bow tie out of a piece of old pipe cleaner, so I looked extremely smart.

'You'd better hide in my pocket while we're in town,' Jonny said as we walked to the bus stop.

'Why?' I asked feeling a little annoyed that I'd have to hide my rather nice bow tie.

'Well, It's very rare for a stick man to come to life and I don't want you to be kidnapped.'

'Don't you mean sticknapped?' I asked giggling.

Jonny shook his head and bundled me into his pocket, where I crouched, not sure what to do. I did pop my head out as we walked around the shops though, and I made sure my bow tie was showing over the edge of the pocket. When we stopped off at the Debenhams café Jonny said I could come out for a little bit. So I jumped out and sat in the centre of a doughnut, eating a neat circle around the middle. "Delicious,' I said, my face covered in sugar.

'So?' I said to Jonny once we got home, 'what new activities can we do to keep busy over the next few weeks?'

'Hmmm' said Jonny as he put tea bags into the new orange teapot, 'let's look on the computer for some ideas.' So, once Jonny's cup and my thimble of tea were ready I sat on Jonny's shoulder and we did a little research.

This book is all about the activities we tried and explains how we got on with them. Some went well, some not so well, my bottom got stuck in things and, most alarmingly, I WAS kidnapped!!!!! Read on to find out more.

ACTIVITY NUMBER 1

Make Mr Squishy heads

'Right', said Jonny, 'activity number one is making Mr Squishy heads'.

'Well, it sounds very good, but what is a Mr Squishy head?' I asked.

Jonny explained what it was all about.

Equipment needed

Two balloons per person

Bag of flour

Scissors

Pen

METHOD

One - *take one of the balloons and blow it up, then deflate it. (This softens the rubber a bit.)*

14

Two - *fill the deflated balloon with flour using the funnel then tie a knot in the neck of the balloon to stop any flour escaping.*

Three - *pick up the second balloon, cut most of the neck off, and then stretch this balloon over the flour filled first balloon. (This makes it much stronger and less likely to explode.)*

Four - *Once both balloons are in place, it's time to decorate the squishy head.*

How it went for us

Jonny read out the method to me and I jumped up and down before hunting around the kitchen for the items. Once I'd found them all I lined them up on kitchen table.

'Right,' said Jonny, reading from the instructions, 'you need to blow up one of the balloons.'

I huffed and puffed, fainted twice and fell into an eggcup once as I tried to blow up my balloon. It was no good, I was far too small, and I think I may have very small lungs that don't hold much air. After trying for forty-five minutes, Jonny agreed to help me.

Once the balloon had been inflated and then deflated again, I put the funnel into the balloon and filled it up with flour. We tied the knot and I pressed the balloon with my hand. It was wonderfully squishy.

'Hold on little guy,' said Jonny, 'we need to cover it with another balloon now, let's use this yellow one.' Using the scissors I snipped most of the neck off the second balloon and threw it to one side, Jonny then started stretching the second balloon over the flour filled first one.

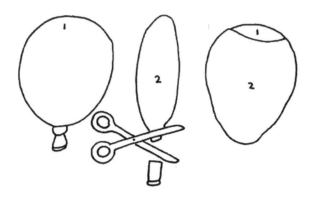

I looked at the cut off neck, which was just lying there on the table. It seemed a shame to waste it, so I decided to turn it into a swimming costume. I wriggled into it and, straight away, found that my bottom was stuck. I stood there looking ridiculous.

'The squishy head is ready for decorating,' said Jonny rolling it towards me. Because my legs were trapped in the rubber tube I couldn't jump out of the way and, as the squishy head rolled into me, I fell over like a bowling pin. Jonny rushed over and picked me up. He couldn't stop laughing as he looked at me trapped in a yellow rubber skirt.

'Hey, rubber skirt making could be one of our future activities,' he said.

I felt my face flush as I struggled to get it off. Jonny said he knew what to do. He then covered me in washing up liquid and put me under the tap.

Eventually, after lots of wet struggling, he managed to pull the rubber skirt off. My mouth was full of the soapy liquid and a bubble came out every time I spoke for at least ten minutes.

Once I was calm and dry he put me back on the table in front of the flour filled balloon. 'Right,' he said, 'now you need to draw a face on it,' he handed me a black pen and I drew a very nice face. It looked like a very friendly Mr Squishy head and I immediately hugged him.

'I'm going to call him Squish Brain Robinson,' I said, as I rolled him into the living room. 'OK,' said Jonny, as he started making one for himself.

I sat on Squish Brain Robinson while we watched TV that evening and I must say he was very comfortable.

Jonny called his Mr Squishy head 'The Flour-Brained Ninja'. His one did look a bit like a ninja as he'd cut a hole in the outer balloon and made it so that the face was peeping through from the inside balloon. What was annoying though was that he kept whispering into the Flour-Brained Ninja's ear and I couldn't hear what he was saying! I hate secrets! I like to know exactly what is going on at all times. Hmmmmmm.

ACTIVITY NUMBER 2

Draw cartoon faces

'I really enjoyed drawing the face onto the Flour-Brained Ninja,' said Jonny the next day, 'and it's given me an idea for activity number two, let's draw cartoon faces.'

I nodded and Jonny got lots of pieces of paper and two newly sharpened pencils ready.

'Right,' he said, giving me one of the pencils, 'there are lots of ways to draw cartoon faces but let's just start by doing different outlines for the heads and then see what characters we think of.' He then drew lots of different shapes onto the paper.

He drew a circle, a square, an egg, a pear, a rectangle and a triangle. I copied and we sat there looking at our pages of shapes.

'Shall I turn one into a face?' I asked.

'Yes, turn them all into faces,' said Jonny. I looked at the shapes for a while, waiting for ideas to flow into me, then got to work creating my own funny cartoon faces. I was struggling a bit for ideas so Jonny showed me this book with different examples of eyes,

noses and mouths in it.

A page from Jonny's book

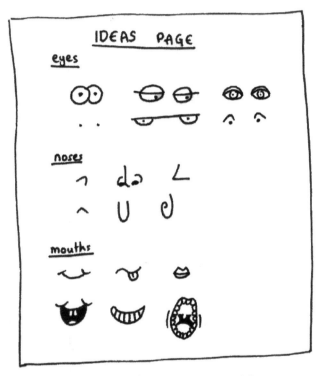

On the next page is what I came up with.

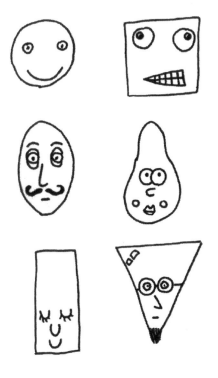

I was quite pleased with my drawings, especially my triangle head so I decided to do a big version of Mr Triangle on a new piece of paper.

This is what Jonny's cartoon faces looked like.

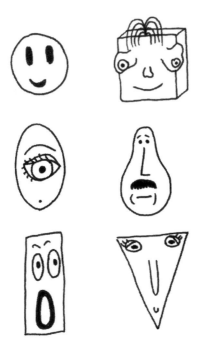

'Yours are kind of strange,' I said as I glanced over.

'Well, strange is better than boring,' Jonny said as he drew hair onto his rather alarming cube head.

'Anyway, I think your triangle head is very, very strange,' he said. I smiled and carried on with my big version.

Once we'd finished we placed all our pictures on the table. They looked really good, especially my large triangle head.

'I think we should display these,' said Jonny. He then went and put them in the front window so that anyone walking along the street could see them. We giggled with delight once they were in place and hid behind the curtain so we could see people's reactions when they looked at them.

A woman came along. She stopped when she got to our house and stared at the pictures for a long time before walking away rather quickly.

That evening we snuggled down next to Squish Brain Robinson and The Flour-Brained Ninja, and watched YouTube films about people drawing cartoons. They were quite good but we liked our own the best.

One week later we were in the garden when our neighbour Jeremy Mothballs popped his head over the fence.

'Did you know,' said Jeremy, 'that a strange man has been hanging around outside your house?'

I looked at Jonny and Jonny looked at me. 'Who could it be?' we said.

'I don't know,' said Jeremy, 'but he keeps staring at the pictures in the window.'

Jonny bit his fingernails, 'I'd forgotten that our cartoon faces were still on display,' he said. It was all very mysterious and a chill ran though me.

'What if he wants to take our drawings?' I said.

'I think we should take the pictures down for a bit,' said Jonny,' rushing into the house.

'So', said Jeremy Mothballs, turning to me, 'shall we have a game of squirt bottle?' I nodded and he filled two bottles with water, he handed one of the bottles to me and we leapt about as we tried to squirt each other. It was great fun and I ended up drenched.

'I'd better get dried,' I said to Jeremy before running into the house and rolling around on a tea towel.

'I think it's time for some conundrum puzzles,' said Jonny later, 'lets make activity number three puzzles. We agreed and shook hands.

'The rule is that we have to find six conundrum puzzles each and then test each other,' he said.

'Brilliant,' I replied, I am looking forward to it already.

ACTIVITY NUMBER 3

Conundrum Puzzles

I hid myself away for two days, looking for good conundrums that I know Jonny wouldn't get. After a lot of research I came up with the six best ones I could find.

Once we were both ready, we turned the lounge into a quiz show room.

We got two chairs and arranged them so they faced each other. I was going to ask the questions first so I sat in the questioner's chair. Jonny sat opposite in the answerer's chair. He had a little bell in his hand ready to shake if he knew the answer.

I cleared my throat and the quiz began. Here are the questions I asked.

One – *What falls but never breaks?*

Two – *What belongs to you but others use it more than you do?*

Three – *The more you take away, the larger it becomes. What is it?*

Four - *what kind of stones are never found in the ocean?*

Five – *what month has 28 days?*

Six - *which word is spelt incorrectly in the dictionary?*

Well, before I give you the answers I'll tell you how Jonny got on trying to answer them.

Overall he did terribly. Heehee

He kept ringing the bell and then giving the **wrong** answer, which was rather amusing. He said that a marshmallow falls but never breaks (which may be true but it wasn't the answer I had so I couldn't accept it.) He said that the answer to number three was 'your mind' ??????, and he said the answer to number six was 'pin'... ((wrong), he said it should be spelt with two n's (NO)).

He got number five one twelfth right, so his total score was one twelfth.

Here are the right answers.

One - temperature (night and rain are also acceptable answers. Marshmallows is not acceptable)

Two - your name

Three - a hole

Four - dry stones

Five - all of them

Six - incorrectly

How did you do? Did you beat Jonny?

Next we swapped places and I had a go at ringing the bell. It was actually really fun to ring so I rang it several times before the game even began.

Here are the questions that Jonny asked me.

One - What time is it when a clock strikes thirteen times?

Two - what has a head and a tail but not legs?

Three - why are teddy bears never hungry?

Four - The more you have of me the less you see. Who am I?

Five - Forwards I'm heavy, but backwards I'm not. What am I?

Six - Say my name and I disappear. Who am I?

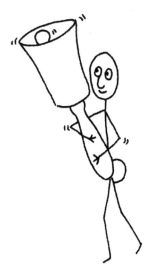

Well, I didn't actually do that well. In fact I got none out of six.

Oh dear.

I did complain though, as my answer to number two, a no legged dog, was technically correct. Jonny agreed and gave me half a point.... Which made me the winner. **YIPEEE**

Here are the actual answers.

One- *time to get a new clock*

Two - *a penny*

Three - *because they're always stuffed.*

Four - *darkness*

Five -*a ton*

Six - *silence*

Did you get more than none right? If you did, then you are extremely clever, possibly even a genius.

We were just celebrating with popcorn when there was a knock at the door. Jonny went to answer it and I followed him to see who was there.

There standing at the door was a very strange looking man with a triangle shaped head. I kind of recognized him but I wasn't sure where from, then I realised that his head looked a bit like the triangle cartoon face I'd drawn the week before.

'Hello, I'm Professor Termite,' he said, 'I would like to ask why was there was picture of me in your window?'

Jonny's mouth fell open.

'Um It wasn't you, it was just a funny cartoon face,' he said.

'You think my face is funny?' said the man. There was a long silence then the professor caught sight of me. He stared and his eyes started blinking as if he couldn't believe it. 'What on earth is THAT?' he asked, pointing my way. I opened my mouth wide then quickly ran back into the sitting room and hid behind a book on the shelf.

'Just a mouse,' said Jonny, starting to shut the door.

'That's the strangest thing I've ever seen,' said Professor Termite, 'I'd love to do some experiments on it.'

'Oh, um, sorry but I'm very busy, I must go,' said Jonny, pushing the door shut.

I crept out from behind the book and we both hid under our orange blanket until the morning.

ACTIVITY NUMBER 4

Marble Shooter Box Game

We didn't see the strange Professor man at all over the next week so we sort of forgot all about him and decided to get on with our activities.

'I've got a brilliant idea for today,' said Jonny as I sat down to breakfast one week later.

'Oh good,' I said trying to fit a whole cheerio into my mouth at once. 'What is it?'

Jonny got something out of the cupboard. 'We'll be needing these,' he said with a big smile on his face. He then held up a string bag with at least ten marbles in it! 'Ta da!'

'Yippee,' I said, jumping up. 'I love marbles.'

Jonny rolled one over to me and it went straight past me so I ran after it, giggling. In the end I caught it and tried to pick it up but it was so heavy that I couldn't quite manage it so I just sat on it and rolled about a bit instead.

'Today's activity is the Marble Shooter Box Game.' He said.

My eyes widened, 'that game sounds amazing,' I said, rubbing my hands together. 'What do we do?'

METHOD

Equipment

A few marbles

One shoebox

Scissors

Pens

Method

One - take the lid off the shoebox and turn it upside down.

Two - cut some holes in the box so that there are a series of open doors along the bottom.

Three - write a number above each door, for scoring.

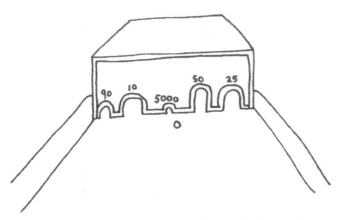

Jonny set up the box and put it at the far and of the table. He then put rolled up towels along the edges of the table, to stop any marbles falling onto the floor.

The whole thing looked really good and I was more than a little excited. I started doing a series of stretches and warm up exercises, ready for the game.

We decided to have five rolls each to see who could get the highest score.

Results

Jonny went first and missed completely. Heeeheee

Then I had a go and missed completely.

Hmmmmmm!

'This is too hard,' said Jonny. He picked up the box and made all the doors a bit wider. 'Right, let's start again.'

This time we actually managed to roll some marbles into the doors. Rolling was difficult for me as

I had to use both hands and all my effort, but in the end my score was 75. Jonny's score was 25.

'I'm the winner,' I sang as I danced about in celebration. Then I had the brilliant idea of going inside the shoebox. I crawled in through the biggest door and stood inside. It was amazing, like a strange room with marbles in it. I stayed in there for quite a long time, rolling about on my bed of glass balls.

When I eventually came out I was pleased to see that Jonny had got me a thimbleful of blueberry juice and a piece of popcorn. Good old Jonny.

'I wonder if we should learn to make a new snack for our next activity?' said Jonny as we tucked into our popcorn.

'Yes,' I replied, 'we've been having popcorn rather a lot lately, so that sounds like a rather yumalicious idea.'

EXTRA INFORMATION

I slept in the shoebox that night. It made a rather nice little bedroom, although my marble bed was a little lumpy.

ACTIVITY NUMBER 5

Jam sushi rolls

'Konnichiwa,' said Jonny the next morning. I looked at him wondering what was going on. He had put four strange sticks on the table and was wearing a long black dressing gown covered in pictures of gold dragons.

'Um, good morning,' I said, picking up one of the sticks. I held it over my head and waved it around.

'Today, for breakfast, we're having Jam sushi rolls,' said Jonny.

I knew I liked jam, and I quite liked rolling around so I nodded in agreement.

'Umm, sounds good, but what's sushi?' I asked.

'Well,' he said, 'real sushi is a Japanese food,' he paused and pointed at his dressing gown, 'there's usually special rice and other ingredients like seaweed or fish involved, but we haven't got the right ingredients for that so I thought we could make our own sushi style rolls out of bread and jam.'

'Sounds good to me,' I said as I put the stick down. Jonny got a loaf of bread out of the cupboard and put it on the table.

METHOD

One - Cut the crusts off a piece of bread, then roll it with a rolling pin to make it as flat as possible.

Two - Add a thin layer of jam (or ham, cheese, peanut butter etc) to the bread then roll it up.

Three - Cut the roll into slices.

How it went for us.

I enjoyed rolling out the bread and managed to make mine extremely flat. I thought it would be fun to roll up in it like a blanket, so, when Jonny wasn't looking, I lay on the bread and rolled it around myself.

'Oh,' Jonny said a minute later, 'here's one ready to cut up.' He then picked the roll up with me inside!!! I screamed and struggled about until he saw my little arms sticking out of the top. He unrolled the bread and I jumped out. Phew, that was close.

I decided to be more sensible in my next attempt and, rather than adding myself, I added a neat layer of jam. I rolled the bread up again and Jonny cut it into slices.

We both smiled as we looked at the pleasing spiral shapes on the plate.

'Now you have to eat it with chopsticks,' said Jonny, handing me two of the sticks. Hmmmmm. The sticks were rather long and I discovered that it is very difficult to eat using utensils that are longer than your arms. After twenty-five minutes of struggling Jonny said I could eat it with my hands but in the end, I just ate it with my mouth and I must say it was delicious.

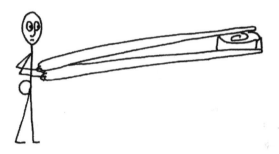

After the meal I had this brilliant idea of using a chopstick as a pole vault and a piece of bread as a crash mat. Grabbing one of the sticks, I ran and used it to project myself really high. When I landed, face first, on the bread mat, I immediately had a mouthful of yummy crumbs, extra bonus.

I practiced the pole vault for most of the day and actually got pretty good at it.

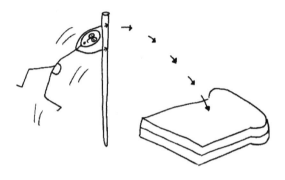

That night I looked up 'Sushi' on the Internet. It didn't look that much like our jam spiral rolls but I decided not to tell Jonny. He seemed to be enjoying the whole Japanese thing and was busy painting Japanese writing onto the side of the shoebox.

ACTIVITY NUMBER 6

Obstacle course

P.S. KIDNAP ALERT!!!!!!

'Well,' said Jonny a few days later, 'It's a nice sunny day, so I've got an outdoor activity planned for this morning.'

'Oh good,' I said, looking out of the window.

'Yes, we're going to make our own obstacle course in the garden.'

'Really, how would we do that?' I asked, rushing to the back door.

METHOD

For this activity you can use any bits and bobs you find in the house or garden to make obstacles. We split the course up into separate activities. Here is how we did it.

Balance - *We laid an old plank down on two bricks to make a balance beam*

Jump - *We put three upside buckets on the floor to jump over.*

Crawl - *Jonny put a mop over two chairs for us to crawl under.*

Throw - *We got four teddies and a cardboard box to throw them into.*

Weave - *Jonny set up a course of hats and shoes for us to zigzag through as quickly as possible.*

Chalk Trail - *On the pavement at the front of the house, we drew a line of chalk to walk along, followed by some circles to jump in before leaping over the finish line.*

These are just a few ideas, but there are millions of different possible obstacles depending up on what you can find.

How it went for us.

I held the stopwatch, as Jonny got ready.

'On your marks, get set....go' I shouted and Jonny set off. He ran along the beam, jumped over the buckets, scrambled under the mop, threw the teddies into the box, zigzagged about then ran through the house and into the front garden. He then ran along the chalk trail, jumped in the circles and leapt over the finish line. I looked at the clock.

'Not bad,' I said, 'only 379 seconds.

Jonny leant over, his hands on his knees, gasping for breath.

'I'm not sure you're going to be able to do it Eric,' he said between breaths, 'I think it's too hard for you.'

'I will do it,' I said, holding my head up high.

So we went through into the back garden, ready for my go.

I wasn't quite as quick as Jonny. It took me forty-seven minutes just to get up onto the plank. Once on I ran along it quite quickly though. Getting over the buckets was very difficult and it took me twenty-eight minutes to get over each one. Going under the mop was very easy and I actually did that a lot quicker than Jonny had. The teddies were quite a struggle, but I did quite well on the zigzag walk. The chalk trail was OK, but the circles were a bit too far apart. Eventually I jumped over the finish line, extremely pleased and proud to have actually finished the course.

'Two hours and sixteen minutes,' said Jonny looking at the stopwatch as I sat down on the floor, exhausted.

'I might make my own obstacle course with very small things to crawl under,' I said, 'I think I would win then.'

'Good idea,' said Jonny as he popped inside to get us drinks. I lay down by the finish line to rest and started thinking about what I could use for my obstacle course.

Then, suddenly, everything went black!! I wasn't sure what was happening, as it was so dark, but it felt like I was being bundled into a box. A box that started moving, as if it were being carried.

'Jonny!' I shouted, but no one seemed to hear.

I sat, shaking, in the darkness as I realized I was

being taken away.

ACTIVITY NUMBER 7

Colourful Flower Experiment

'Well, well, well,' said a strange voice as the lid of

the box opened and a man peered in. I recognized

him straight away as professor Termite, the man who had come round to the house a couple of weeks ago.

'Let me go,' I said.

'You are too interesting to let go,' he said as he picked me up and looked at me. 'What is this big bump on you?' he asked, 'is it a great big enormous bottom?'

I went bright red and wriggled around. 'Get off me.' I said.

Professor Termite started laughing, 'Oh dear big bum man, I think you would look a lot better if we cut it off, don't you?'

I started shaking. Suddenly I rather liked my big bum, even though I'd been complaining about it ever since I was born.

He then shoved me in a test tube that was a little too small for me and I was immediately stuck.

'That's handy,' said Professor Termite, 'that will stop you going anywhere while I do all my other jobs and experiments.'

I looked around the room and saw hundreds of test tubes in stands with different things in them. There were mixing sticks, Bunsen burners and bottles of vinegar everywhere. My test tube was in a rack with three other tubes, each of them containing a single white flower standing in water.

'I'm doing an experiment with these,' said Professor Termite, tapping the flowers. He then got some bottles of flood colouring and put lots of drops of different food colouring into the water of each of the three test tubes. 'These white flowers should change colour once the water is taken up into the petals, wont that be interesting?' he said.

'I need to go home, ' I said, 'Jonny will be so worried.'

'Yes, I know, but you're so unusual I think I can make a lot of money out of you, can you sing? Perhaps we could make you into a YouTube sensation, once the bum has gone of course.'

'I don't want to do it,' I said, struggling about a bit.

'Unfortunately,' said Professor Termite, 'I've got a lot to do today so we might have to sort your bottom out tomorrow.' He then got on with all sorts of strange experiments for what seemed like several hours. Most of the procedures seemed to involve putting a drop of vinegar on different things.

I kept looking at the white flowers and, after a few hours, they started to change colour. The edges of the petals were turning purple, red and blue. They actually looked really good but I was too worried to be amazed. In fact my heart was beating very fast and my hands were holding tightly on to the edge of the tube.

'Right, I'm finished for today,' said Professor Termite eventually, 'I'll be back in the morning with my best scissors. The good news it that tonight will be your last night with that embarrassing bum.'

I heard the Professor leave and lock the door and I started looking around the room for ways to escape. I noticed that one of the windows was slightly open but it was quite high up and probably too high for me to climb out. Besides I was stuck fast in the tube.

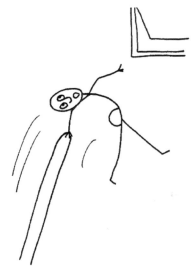

I started rocking back and forth, making the test tubes move, I did it faster and faster until the test tubes rack fell and all the tubes smashed. I grabbed a mixing stick and used it to try and pole vault out of the window. Unfortunately I missed and splattered onto the glass before sliding down onto the windowsill.

I tried again and again until I flew out and landed onto the pavement. Hooray!! I was bruised and sore, but I was free.

I limped about the streets until I saw a little corner shop I recognized. I knew the way home from there. When I got home I slipped through the letterbox and looked for Jonny. He was lying on the floor crying.

When he saw me he jumped up and hugged me for a long time. I was so happy to see him and a tear of relief rolled down my cheek.

'Where've you been?' he asked, 'I've been looking for you for hours.'

I told him all about the kidnap and he shook his head in shock.

I slept in Jonny's pocket that night.

ACTIVITY NUMBER 8

Make a Path based board game

Over the next few days Jonny kept the curtains

closed in case Professor Termite came looking for me.

He also made me a special pair of bottom protecting

underpants out of tin foil, in case the professor

turned up with scissors.

Neither of us felt like going out, we just wanted to

hide, and luckily Jonny had an idea for a brilliant stay

inside activity. 'Let's make our own board games,' he said.

I agreed as it sounded fun but there was a problem! I was not at all comfy in my tin foil underpants. They were scratchy, cold and kept digging in when I bent my legs. I told Jonny and he said I could take them off. Phew.

We got to work on our games.

METHOD

Equipment

Big piece of card or paper

Dice

Pens

Counters (to move round the game)

Other bits of card or paper for forfeits, challenges, collected items etc.

Ideas

Method

One - *Draw a path with lots of positions to land on. These could be squares, circles, stepping stones, clouds or anything you can think off.*

Two - *Have messages on some of the positions, these could be to do forfeits or challenges, move forward or backward instructions, or benefits, such as collect an item card to use later in the game.*

Three - *Start designing the game.*

How it went for us

We spent a long time on our games. My game was called 'ANT COLLECTOR' and was all about landing on the 'collect ant' positions; it took me twelve hours to complete (lots of tea breaks) and was actually very good.

In my ANT COLLECTOR game I decided to have a loop where you keep going round the board until you have collected 6 ants

We played my game and **I won!!!!!!!**

Jonny made a strange game that was meant to be about static electricity. In his game, the first to the finish line is the winner.

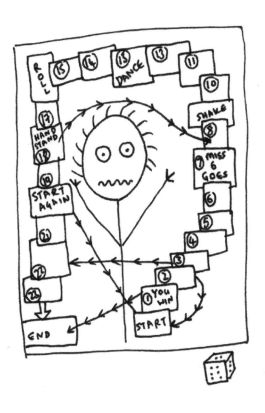

Jonny won the STATIC ELECTIRICITY game because

I landed on the 'miss 6 goes' square. Hmmmmmm.

ACTIVITY NUMBER 9

Funny Iced biscuits

'You know,' said Jonny a few days later, 'I think we should make some iced biscuits, to celebrate our brilliant board games.'

I agreed and we got busy with the icing sugar.

Ingredients

Pack of plain biscuits

2 cups of icing sugar

2 tbsp of water

Food colouring (we used yellow)

Gummy sweets (we used fried egg sweets and strawberry laces)

Method

One - *Put the icing sugar into a bowl and add enough water to make a spreadable paste. Add a drop of food colouring.*

Two - *Spread the icing onto a biscuit*

Three - *add the sweets.*

We made fifteen altogether and they looked excellent. For decoration we used two fried egg shaped sweets to make eyes then added a bit of strawberry lace to make a big smiley yummy face.

YIPPEEE

We decided to eat one straight away, and save the rest for another day. They were delicious, especially the yolks from the gummy eggy eyes!

ACTIVITY NUMBER 10

Road Trip Scavenger Hunt

'I've been thinking,' said Jonny the next day, 'we've been hiding away in the house all week and I think it would be good for us to get away for a few days.'

'Do you mean a holiday?' I said, starting to tingle.

'Yes,' said Jonny. I immediately ran upstairs to pack. I don't really have many belongings so it didn't take long. I just threw my sweet wrapper suit, pipe cleaner bow tie and tin foil underpants into a small sandwich bag and I was ready.

Jonny put two sleeping bags and some snacks into the back of the funny orange van and we set off.

'Um, where are we going' I asked as I climbed up onto the dashboard.

Jonny looked at me, 'I don't know,' he said. 'I forgot to think about that but I have got a holiday activity for you.'

He handed me a piece of paper with a list of things on it. Then he gave me a small pencil and told me to tick off any items I see from the car window.

The list

City items

Bus

Dog

Car Number plate with an X

Person with tall boots

Person talking on a phone

Flashing red light

Green traffic light

Food store

A police car

Suburb items

Someone on a bike

A hanging basket of flowers

A School

A fish and chip shop

A supermarket

A zebra crossing

A motorbike

A green car

Countryside items

A sheep

A cow

A petrol station

A tractor

A pond or lake

A horse

A lorry

I eagerly studied the list and started ticking things off straight away.

After two hours of driving I'd ticked off over half the items.

'Have you decided where we're going yet?' I asked Jonny as I put a tick by the word sheep for the forty-seventh time.

'Yes Eric,' said Jonny, 'I think we should go to that forest.' He pointed to an area of trees in the distance.

'Hooray,' I said, pleased that the end of the long journey was in sight.

Once we arrived Jonny parked the van and we climbed into the back. We unwrapped our sandwiches and funny iced biscuits and had a lovely meal. We were quite tired after the long journey so we got into the sleeping bags and had a good sleep.

I was woken early by the sound of birds the next day.

ACTIVITY NUMBER 11

Tree Hugging!!!! (Yes we actually did this)

Location

Woodland

Equipment

Blindfold

We got out of our sleeping bags and went into the forest. I saw a stone covered in moss and jumped onto it, feeling the cool mossy carpet under my feet. I smiled up at Jonny as he started cooking some scrambled eggs on a little gas stove.

'We need a good breakfast ready for a busy day in the forest,' he said, mixing up the eggs in the frying pan.

I looked at the enormous trees all around us, everything was so green and there was a delicious smell of wood mixed with scrambled eggs.

As we ate, Jonny told me that he had a brilliant t idea for the first forest activity.

'What is it?' I asked as I sat down on a pebble.

'Well, It sounds a bit strange, but I promise it will be fun.'

I raised my eyebrow and looked at him.

'It's tree hugging,' he said.

I grinned; tree hugging sounded fun although I was a bit worried about finding a tree small enough to get my arms round.

'I might hug that one,' I said, pointing to a nearby baby tree.

'No, no, I pick the tree for you, in fact, you wont see it until long after you've hugged it.'

'What?????'

Jonny explained how it all worked.

METHOD

One – *A person is blindfolded in an area with lots of trees.*

Two - *the other person chooses a tree and leads the blindfolded person to it.*

Three - *Once at the tree, the blindfolded tree hugger feels the tree and has to try and remember the smell, shape and texture of it.*

Four - *After that, the hugger is led back to the starting point.*

Five – *The blindfold is removed and the hugger has to go and find the tree they had hugged.*

'Sounds fun,' I said, leaping up, 'can I be blindfolded first?'

How it went for us

Jonny nodded and got a tiny blindfold out of his pocket before leading me to a tree. It was so strange staggering about in darkness but Jonny kept hold of my hand. I kept stumbling over bumps in the ground and nearly banging in to things but, after a few minutes Jonny said, 'We're here, we've arrived at your tree.'

I moved my small hands forward and felt bark, I held my arms out and did actually manage to hug the tree, although I couldn't quite get my arms right round it. I smelt it and it smelt like... hmmm, I'm not sure... perhaps bark?

After a while I was led back to my starting point. I took the blindfold off and then ran about looking for my tree. I knew it was pretty thin so that helped. I dashed about hugging a few small trees and then I thought I recognised the feel of one.

'Is this it?' I asked

'Amazing Eric,' said Jonny, doing a strange thumbs up movement.

Then it was Jonny's turn to put a blindfold on.

It was quite hard leading Jonny as he is much

bigger than me, so, in the end I just ran in front of

him shouting, 'forward, turn left, turn right, watch

out for stones.' Eventually I found a suitable tree and

Jonny hugged it. I then led him back to the van. He

carefully removed the blindfold then went off to try

and identify his tree.

PROBLEM

There was one little problem. The tree Jonny hugged looked very similar to most of the other trees in the area and I couldn't remember which one it was.

'Is it this one?' Jonny kept saying.

'Ummm, no not that one,' I said, although I had no idea.

'I give up,' said Jonny after his twenty-ninth guess.

'I think it was this one,' I said, nervously pointing at a tree very near the van.

'Oh, my tree,' said Jonny, hugging it again.

(I don't think it was the same tree but he didn't seem to realize. Eeeeeek)

After the activity we went for a walk. We found a stream and tried to cross it by jumping from one stone to another. It was quite fun, although I got rather wet.

ACTIVITY NUMBER 12

Torch Hide and Seek

We played around in the forest all day and Jonny even made a little bonfire, upon which we cooked marshmallows. A M A Z I N G L Y   Y U M

About two hours after that the sun disappeared and it started to get dark. We looked up at the moon, which cast a slight silvery light over us. I breathed in the lovely bonfire smell and leant back on a little bed I'd made out of leaves. I then closed my eyes and had a small snooze. I was just in the middle of a dream about having no bottom when Jonny woke me up by shining a torch in my eyes.

'Come on Eric', he said, it's time for activity number twelve.'

I stood up and stretched, 'what are we going to do?' I asked.

'We're going to play torch hide and seek' he said, suddenly shining the torch all around. It lit up the trees and strange shadows jumped about. I felt a wave of fear wobble though me.

'How do we play?' I said, nervously looking around the darkening forest.

METHOD

One - *Find an area that is darkish, safe to run around in and has lots of hiding places.*

Two - *Decide who it going to be 'it' and give them the torch.*

Three - *The person who is ''it' counts to sixty while everyone else hides.*

Four - *Then they start to look for the other players, using the torch to help them. When they find someone, they have to shine the light on their face and call out their name.*

'OK,' I said, looking around for good hiding places. I'll hide first'. Jonny nodded then started to count to sixty. I bounded across the leafy forest floor and dived behind a tree, my heart was beating fast as I found an excellent hiding place under a raised root. I chewed my lip and kept pressing my fingers together as I crept into the little space.

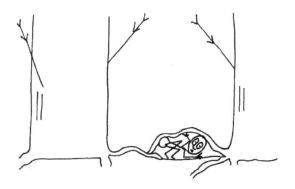

I shuddered all over as I saw the light swooping about causing shadows to leap towards me.

It took ages but finally the flashlight landed on me, and my name was called out. I leapt out from under the root, smiling. 'It took you quite a long time to find me,' I said.

'Yes, the problem is, you look just like a twig,' said Jonny. Hmmmm, I'm not sure I like the sound of that.

Then it was Jonny's turn to hide. I looked for him

for seventy minutes but he was nowhere to be found.

I was getting very tired and, even though I only had a

mini torch, my arms were starting to ache. I was

getting a bit fed up and decided to have a break and

sleep in the van before continuing the search in the

morning.

I felt a little bit guilty as I made may way back to

the van as I knew it would mean Jonny would be

hiding all night, but it was sort of his own fault for finding such a good hiding place.

As I climbed into my sleeping bag I heard a strange noise. It was someone snoring! I went to investigate and yes, it was Jonny, he was fast asleep next to me. I shone the light in his face and shouted 'found you,' until the snoring stopped. Then we both snuggled down for the night.

The next morning we decided to go home. We sang funny made up songs all the way back to 41 Brooklands Avenue.

As soon as we got home there was a knock on the door. It was Jeremy Mothballs.

'Hello,' he said, 'I just wanted you to let you know that that strange man with the triangular head has been hanging around again, I think he's looking for Eric.'

I froze and Jonny put me into his pocket.

'When was he here?' asked Jonny.

'Yesterday, and the day before, he keeps looking around the front garden, he was even poking around behind the plant pots next to your front door.'

Jonny thanked Jeremy for letting him know and we went into the lounge and pulled the curtains.

'Don't worry Eric,' said Jonny as I popped my head out of his pocket, 'We'll think of a way to get rid of him.'

ACTIVITY NUMBER 13

Talent show

The next day we decided to have a talent show.

'Let's do an act together,' I said to Jonny as he checked that the curtains were thoroughly closed.

'OK,' he replied, 'but we'll need an audience.'

'Let's ask Jeremy Mothballs,' I said, 'perhaps he can do an act too.'

'Good idea,' said Jonny, going off to ask him.

It was arranged that Jeremy would come round at seven o'clock that evening. That meant that we had nine hours to get everything ready.

Our Act

After a lot of discussion we decided to do a comedy routine. As there were two of us we thought it would be good to do a series of doctor doctor jokes. I was going to dress up as the doctor and Jonny would be various patients. We spent several hours getting the jokes and costumes ready before waiting eagerly for Jeremy to arrive.

The Show

The doorbell rang at five minutes to seven. I rushed to open it and was surprised to see Jeremy dressed up as a giant parsnip. He couldn't walk, as there were no leg holes so we carried him into the lounge and lay him on the red rug, which we were using at the stage. We sat on the sofa, ready to watch his performance.

Jeremy's performance

We watched Jeremy lying on the floor for a while wondering what was going to happen. Suddenly he started singing.

'I am the ghost of a carrot,' he sang. He repeated this six times.

Jonny and I looked at each other. We weren't sure if it was meant to be funny or not. Jonny's shoulders were shaking as if he were trying not to laugh which made me want to laugh too.

Suddenly Jeremy rolled over and sang, 'Ooooooo wooooooooo,' in a funny voice, and then he sort of sat up and started swaying from side to side. After a while he stopped and we got the feeling his act was over.

Jonny and I clapped nervously as Jeremy climbed out of his outfit. He was smiling proudly as he sat next to us on the sofa.

'Very good,' said Jonny.

'Thanks, I've been practicing for an hour,' said Jeremy.

Then it was our turn.

Our Performance

I put on my doctors coat and stethoscope and sat on a chair. Then Jonny came in dressed as a patient. He changed outfits between each joke to make it a bit funnier. Here are the jokes we came up with.

Doctor Doctor, my nose runs and my feet smell

I think you might have been built upside down

Doctor Doctor I think I'm invisible

Next please

*Doctor Doctor, what can I do, everyone thinks
I'm a liar?*

I find that very hard to believe

Doctor, Doctor, I feel like a pair of curtains

Pull yourself together

*Doctor, Doctor, I've got a bit of lettuce sticking
out of my ear*

*Oh dear, and I think that's just the tip of the
iceberg*

Doctor Doctor, I feel like a parsnip

Don't get yourself into a stew

By the end of the show Jeremy was lying face down
on the sofa with tears of laughter streaming down his
face. Jonny and I grinned and gave each other a high
five.

'That was the funniest thing ever,' said Jeremy. 'I
wish I'd done comedy now, instead of a serious play.'
Jonny and me looked at each other and smiled.

After that we all shared a bowl of popcorn and watched YouTube films about talking dogs.

'Good night,' said Jeremy later, as he carefully folded up his parsnip costume and went home.

'See you soon,' we said and I put the stethoscope away.

ACTIVITY NUMBER 14

Salt Dough Sculptures of Ourselves

We were sitting with the Flour-Brained Ninja and Squish Brain Robinson, watching a little TV the next morning, when Jonny suddenly jumped up.

'I've got an idea for today's activity,' he said, rushing into the kitchen. I followed him, wondering what was going on.

'We need flour, salt and paint,' said Jonny, hunting through the cupboards.

'What are we doing?' I asked, climbing up onto the worktop.

'We're going to make salt dough sculptures of ourselves,' said Jonny.

I leapt up and punched the air with excitement.

'Yeeeees!!!' (Don't look at it.)

SALT DOUGH ACTIVITY

Ingredients

1 cup of salt

2 cups flour

Three quarters of a cup of water

Method

One - *mix the flour and salt together in a large bowl.*

Two - *mix the water in until the mixture becomes a thick dough.*

Three - *put the dough mixture on a breadboard and knead it until smooth.*

Four - *Once you have a nice lump it's time to make your sculpture.*

Five - *Once ready, pop your sculpture into the oven (more on this later)*

You could make just your head, your whole body or something completely different. The brilliant thing is that it is up to you what you do with your lovely doughy lump of joy.

How it went for us

The mixing went well but I found the kneading rather difficult. My hands a little bit on the small side so I could only knead a marble-sized bit at a time. In the end Jonny put a very small piece at the edge of the breadboard for me to knead and he did the rest. Soon both pieces of dough were ready and we mixed them together to make a nice big lump.

I decided to do a life size full body sculpture of myself. This worked well for me because I am small, but will only work for people who are smaller than the inside of an oven, unless you do it in pieces and glue them together later.

Jonny helped me to roll worms of dough. These became my body, legs and arms, we then did a nice round face and I drew my rather nice expression on it with a stick. Jonny then attached a large lump onto the bottom area.

'Hey, hey,' I said, frowning, 'my bottom's not that big!'

'I think it is,' said Jonny looking at me from behind.

'No, no, it's half that size,' I said, trying to twist my head round to look at my own behind.

Jonny took some of the dough off, it still looked big but I agreed to go along with it. I began to wonder if my bottom was even bigger than I thought!

Soon it was finished and we put it in the oven.

COOKING THE DOUGH

Once your sculpture is ready, put it into the oven at 180C. The amount of time needed to bake it depends on the size. Keep checking it to make sure it doesn't get burnt.

P.S. Get a grown up to help with the oven bit.

After that Jonny made a sculpture of his face.

'No, no, the nose is much too small,' I said, looking at it, 'you need to make it at least two times bigger.'

Jonny sighed and added a little more dough to the face before sliding his into the oven too.

We then had a drink of pomegranate juice and waited for the creations to be ready. I tried to eat a little bit of the leftover dough but it was disgusting and I spat it out straight away. **SOoOOO SaLty YuKky.**

Once the dough was baked we got our sculptures out of the oven and waited for them to cool. They looked really good although Jonny's nose had spread out quite a lot and looked very funny.

My model was brilliant though, and, once it was cold I painted it the exact same colour as me. When I lay down next to it you could hardly tell who was who.

Jonny painted his sculpture too and we left them on the kitchen table to dry overnight.

The next morning when we came into the kitchen we went straight over to have a look at them.

'They look really good,' I said, admiring my handy work.

'They do,' said Jonny, 'hey, shall we put them outside at the front of the house so that Jeremy can see them when he sets off for work?' He might even think it's us in the garden.

'Good idea,' I said, I'm not sure he'll be fooled by your head on it's own without a body though'.

We put the items out in the front garden and then ran inside to look out of the window. Jeremy always set off at around nine o'clock so we knew we'd only have to wait a few minutes. We were just peering around the curtains, looking out for him when we both saw something that made us freeze.

There, creeping around in our front garden was PROFESSOR TERMITE!!!!

I stared at Jonny, Jonny stared at me, and then we both peered at the professor as he started coming towards the house. Suddenly he saw the salt dough model of me.

'Noooooo,' he shouted, 'you've died!' he then picked up the sculpture and looked at it. He wiped a tear from his face as he stared at the little salt dough man.

He then ran off shouting 'I can't believe it, the stick man is dead, my chances of fame and fortune are over.' We then saw him throw the sculpture over a fence and SPLASH; it landed in someone's garden pond. Professor Termite then disappeared around a corner.

A few minutes' later Jeremy mothballs walked past. He didn't notice the 'Jonny face' sculpture at all.

'Well, I don't think we need to worry about professor Termite any more,' said Jonny. He opened the curtains and sun streamed into the room. The curtains had been shut for a long time and it was really strange to have a light living room again. I smiled and moved to sit in a ray of sunshine. 'I think I need to make a new sculpture though, as mine is now lying at the bottom of a pond.' I said as the sun warmed me.

ACTIVITY NUMBER 15

Cress heads

Two days later Jonny woke me early. 'Eric Trum, come downstairs, I've got another activity for us to do.'

I rolled over and went back to sleep for a while.

'Come on Eric,' he continued, 'it's going to be extremely fun.'

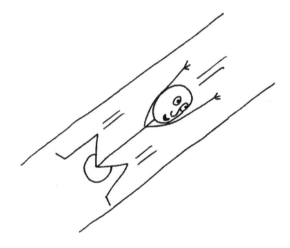

I slowly emerged from under the covers and slid down the banister. 'Good morning,' I said, entering the kitchen.

Jonny was cooking scrambled eggs in the kitchen and had put all the empty eggshells into eggcups.

'Um, I think you're meant to put full eggs into egg cups,' I said, peering into one.

'No, no, we need these for our next activity, but before we begin, would you like some scrambled eggs?'

'Yes please,' I said, sitting at the table, 'so what is the activity?'

Jonny explained everything.

CRESS HEADS

Ingredients

Eggshells with the tops cut off

Kitchen roll

Cotton wool

Cress seeds

Pen

Instructions

One - *Put the eggshells into eggcups.*

Two - Put a scrunched up piece of wet kitchen roll into each eggshell.

Three - Wet a thin piece of cotton wool and add this on top of the kitchen roll.

Four - Sprinkle cress seeds onto the cotton wool.

Five - draw a funny face on the eggshell.

Six - when the cress has grown, eat it. It may taste good in an egg sandwich.

'Sounds quite good,' I said as I shovelled scrambled egg into my mouth, 'I may draw a large moustache on my egg head, I think that would look quite good.'

'I'm going to make mine extremely realistic,' said Jonny. 'I may even make a nose out of left over salt dough and glue it on, so it looks really 3d.'

We finished our breakfast and got to work.

We wet the kitchen roll and cotton wool and put them in the eggshells, and then we got the packet of cress seeds. I was just tearing it open when I felt a massive sneeze coming on. I tried to hold it in, but I couldn't and sneezed the biggest sneeze ever! As I sneezed my hands flew into the air and cress seeds flew everywhere.

'Oh dear,' said Jonny, as he scooped as many as he could up and put them into the eggheads.

Then it was time to decorate the eggs. Here's what they looked like.

'They look good,' I said, admiring them, 'but the cress hasn't grown yet.'

Jonny laughed, 'Eric,' he said, 'it will take a few days for the cress to grow.'

'Oh, I was hoping to eat it for my dinner today.' I said, rubbing my tummy.

Jonny smiled, 'well, it will be fun waiting.'

'Yes, I suppose so,' I said, moving my moustache egghead to the windowsill.

The next morning I ran straight to the egg heads and guess what, there were little tiny white shoots coming out of the seeds.

ACTIVITY NUMBER 16

Pipe Cleaner Ninja

As I lay in bed the next day, I felt a strange tingling on my head. I moved my hand up to feel it and was amazed to find…. I was growing a hair!!!!

I couldn't believe it. I'd always been bald so it was very exciting. I started thinking about hairstyles I could have. Wondering if I could put a roller in it, or if I could stick it straight up like a Mohican. I drifted off to sleep dreaming of a future life with a hair.

Later that day Jonny appeared with a bag that said 'craft shop' on it. I jumped around with joy before showing him my hair.

'Yes there is something there,' said Jonny examining my head. I grinned as Jonny emptied the contents of his bag onto the kitchen table.

'We're going to make pipe cleaner ninjas,' he said, as pipe cleaners, beads and drinking straws spilled out onto the table.

'Good,' I said, picking up two straws and running around with them, 'so how do we do it?

PIPE CLEANER NINJAS

Equipment

Pipe cleaners

Coloured drinking straws

Large wooden beads (usually available from craft shops)

Pony or other smaller beads

Instructions

One - *Twist three pipe cleaners together to look like this. (Twist the centre a few times to make the body)*

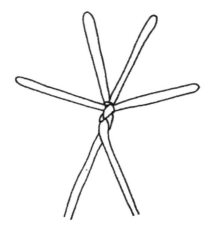

Two - *slide three pony beads over both legs and place over the body.*

Three - Cut drinking straws into eight three-centimetre segments. Slide two segments onto each arm and two segments onto each leg. On the legs, put a pony bead between the segments to make knees.

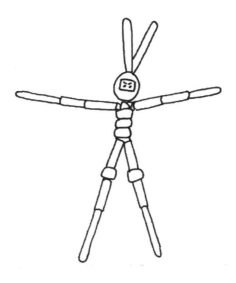

Four - Twist left over pipe cleaner into hands and feet, and wrap the excess around the wrist or ankle to stop the straws from coming off.

Five - Draw a ninja face onto a wooden bead and slide it over the top two pipe cleaners. Cut off the excess pipe cleaner but leave a little bit to make a pony tail and glue this down onto the back of the head.

Six - swords and weapons can be made from extra pipe cleaners.

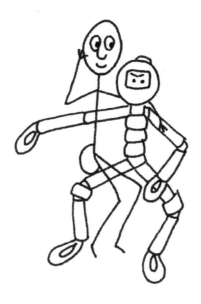

We busily made our Ninjas and guess what!!???
They looked brilliant!

We played ninja chase for six hours, which was rather exciting, although the ninja's were rubbish at chasing. We were so busy playing that we forgot to have lunch.

That night we sat with our ninjas and watched some TV. Then we checked our cress. It was starting to get quite tall and a few pieces even had leaves emerging.

The next morning I woke up early and decided that now that I had a hair I should probably start combing it. I searched around in the bathroom cupboard for a comb and eventually found one that looked like it was a hundred years old. It was rather grubby but I decided that it would have to do and rushed to the mirror ready to groom my hair.

When I looked in the mirror I couldn't believe it. My heart sank and my eyes filled with water. No, it couldn't be true.

If you don't like bad news, just skip this section and go on to activity number 17.

The Bad News

The 'hair' had grown leaves and looked very much like a piece of cress. Oh dear, perhaps I wont be having a lifetime of hair after all.

ACTIVITY NUMBER 17

Make a Soctopus (an Amazing Sock Octopus)

It is Jonny's birthday in exactly one week so the next day I decided to make him a present.

I got up at five in the morning, while Jonny was still fast asleep, and crept into the kitchen. I'd already decided what I wanted to make him and luckily, everything I needed was lying around the house.

SOCTOPUS

Equipment

An old sock

Stuffing

Felt

Glue

Pipe cleaners

Instructions

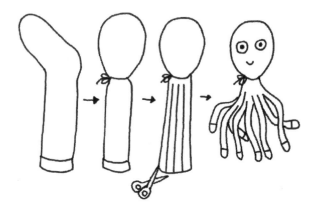

One - Fill the toe bit of the sock with stuffing to make the head.

Two - tie and secure the head with string.

Three - make eyes out of circles of felt and glue them on.

Four - cut the end of the sock, nearly up to the head, to make eight tentacles.

Five (optional) - cut to size and glue a pipe cleaner to the underside of each tentacle, then wrap the *fabric round it and glue shut. (Hot glue works well*

for this - but ask a grown up to help)

TOP TIP - Don't use your mum's best sock

I worked extremely hard for two hours. It was very difficult getting the stuffing in, as I am rather small and I ended up stuck in the fluffy octopus brain for quite a while. I got out in the end and carried on though.

Eventually I closed the last tentacle and the amazing Sock Octopus was born!! It looked absolutely AMAZING and I danced in and out of its tentacles for a while. Then I noticed that it was nearly half past seven, which is when Jonny gets up, so I quickly wrapped the octopus in some purple wrapping paper and hid it behind the sofa. I then did a rather large yawn and went back to bed.

ACTIVITY NUMBER 18

Fireflies

'Quick quick, the cress is ready,' shouted Jonny the next day. I raced downstairs and was amazed to see that each egghead now had a full head of cress hair. I reached up sadly to my feel own 'hair', which was now just a drooping piece of nearly dead cress, flopping in front of my eye.

'Look at my hair,' I said.

'Never mind,' said Jonny, plucking it and eating it.

I was bald again and looked at him in alarm.

'So shall we eat cress for breakfast?' I asked.

'Great idea,' he said.

We then boiled some eggs and had a marvellous

egg and cress sandwich. Rather good.

'So what are we doing today?' I asked as we

finished the washing up.

'Well today we are going to make glowing fireflies, then tonight, when it get's dark, we'll hang them in the garden and they'll look brilliant.'

'I know,' I said, 'let's make them today, then save them to hang in the garden on your birthday next week, perhaps we could even invite a few people round and have a little party?'

Jonny nodded, 'I'd love that,' he said, rubbing his eyes.

As it was sunny, we decided to make them in the garden and took all the equipment outside.

Green bottle Firefly

Equipment

An empty small green fizzy drink bottle

Pipe cleaners

Card and tape

A glow stick

Instructions

One - wrap three pipe cleaners around the middle of the bottle to be the legs

Two - glue a paper rectangle around the top of the centre of the bottle; make sure the head, bottom and tummy are not covered.

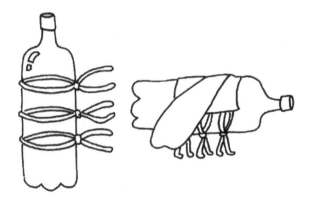

Three - Cut wing shapes out of card and glue these to the top of the body.

Four - Wrap a pipe cleaner around the neck of the bottle to be the antennae

Five - *glue card eyes onto the bottle top, (with the lid on, to check they're in the right position*

Six - *take the lid off and pop in the glow stick*
Seven - *hang from a tree.*

-

How it went for us

Once we'd added all the bits, I thought it would be fun to try and climb into the bottle so I could see what the world looked like from inside a green bug body, but then this happened!! I got stuck!

'Help!' I shouted as I waved my arms and legs around. Suddenly someone threw a bucket of water over me. I gasped for breath as torrents of water poured over my face. Then a second later I saw Jeremy Mothballs. He'd jumped over the fence from next door and was now hitting the wet bottle firefly with a stick.

'Let Eric go,' he shouted at the firefly.

'It's not a real insect,' said Jonny, helping to pull me out.

'Oh, ok,' said Jeremy, hiding the bucket behind his back.

'Do you want a cup of tea?' Jonny said. Jeremy nodded and, once we'd hung the fireflies up in the tree, we all sat down for a drink.

The dangling bugs looked rather good, although mine was now rather wet which made the wings very floppy. We didn't put the glow sticks in yet; we decided to save them for Jonny's birthday.

'The garden's looking nice,' said Jeremy as he sipped his tea. They then had a long chat about plants.

I wonder why there are never any green flowers?' said Jonny looking around the garden. 'I mean you can get flowers in just about every other colour.'

'I don't know,' said Jeremy.

'Perhaps because bees might not notice them,' I said, feeling very clever.

'Of course,' said Jonny, 'I wish there were green flowers though.'

ACTIVITY NUMBER 19

Birthday Decorations

It was the day before Jonny's birthday so I decided to make some decorations. I popped round to Jeremy's house and he agreed to help me. We decided to make paper chains to hang in the garden. I also had this brilliant idea of making some green flowers, as that would really surprise Jonny. I remembered Professor Termite's trick with the food colouring and told Jeremy all about it. He rushed to the shops to get all the equipment.

He soon returned with 20 white carnation flowers, a bottle of green food colouring, and lots of different coloured paper.

We put the flowers in a vase of water and added sixty drops of green colouring. The website said that it would take about 24 hours for the flowers to go green so we put them on the windowsill and got on with the paper chains.

Paper Chains

METHOD

One - *cut paper into lots of pieces that are the same size. We cut our to be 2.5cm by 20cm.*

Two - *tape the ends together to make a loop.*

Three - *Place the second strip of paper through the loop and tape that one up too.*

Four - *Carry on until you have a very long chain.*

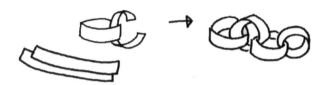

Once the chain was ready we went into the garden and hung it from the tree. Everything was looking very good and I was mega excited about the birthday party.

ACTIVITY NUMBER 20

Jonny's Birthday Party

'Happy Birthday,' I shouted the next morning before jumping onto Jonny's shoulder.

Jonny woke up and came downstairs. As soon as he went into the kitchen he saw the present in purple wrapping paper sitting on the kitchen table. He opened it up.

'Wow, a sock octopus, I LOVE it,' he said, immediately bending all its tentacles so it could stand up on the table.

We then had a very special breakfast of funny iced biscuits and chocolate. After that there was a ring on the doorbell. Jonny rushed to answer it.

'Happy birthday,' said Jeremy, holding a big bunch of green flowers.

'Amazing,' Jonny grinned as he took the flowers, 'come in.'

We all had a cup of tea then Jeremy left to go to work. It was all arranged he would come back in the evening for the party.

During the day we watched a little TV. We put the news on and were surprised to see Professor Termite being put into a police van. It turns out he was being arrested for poisoning fresh water fish by throwing salty dough into their pond!

At eight o'clock the party began. We went into the garden and put the glow sticks into the bottle fireflies, making them light up beautifully. We also set up the obstacle course as we thought it would be a fun party activity.

There was a ring on the doorbell and Jonny's friend Firna arrived, as did his brother Jokey Joe, then, a few minutes later Jeremy arrived. He was wearing his parsnip costume so we had to carry him into the garden and put him in a chair.

It was a great party and we had a lot of fun, although Jeremy struggled a little on the obstacle course.

Oh dear

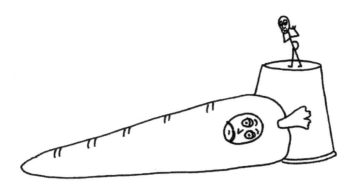

Well that's all for now, but I hope you enjoyed reading about our adventures. Perhaps you may even try some of the activities yourself?

See you next time.

Best wishes

Your Friend

Eric Trum

byeeee.